I'M here

by Peter H. Reynolds

Atheneum Books for Young Readers

New York London Toronto Sydney

Can you hear it?
Voices.
Splashes upon splashes of sound.

I hear it all
like one big noise.
A big drum.
Boom. Boom.

Boom.
Boom.

They are there.

I am here.

Yes, I'm here.
I know I am.

I am here.

With the breeze.
Gentle wind.

I like the soft wind
patting my head.

Tumbling leaf stops at my knee
for a visit.

Sailing paper glides
from the air

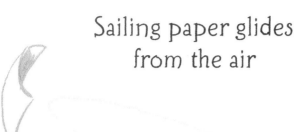

to me!

White rectangle.
How did you find me?

This is not where the paper
wants to be.

No worries, friend.
I'm here.

I make a fold.

 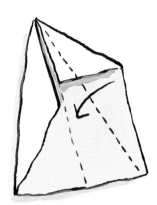 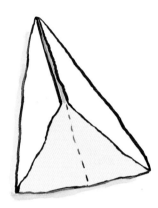

I fold, fold, fold, fold, fold. . . .

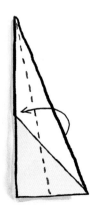 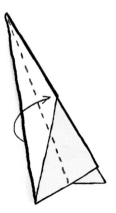 

I'm done.

Ready?

We're off!

Clouds!

Higher!

Higher.

Higher.

And look—
stars!

They sparkle loudly,
like voices on a playground.
Splashes upon splashes of sound.

Loudly I shout:

I'm here!

We've got you!

They've got me!
My paper airplane and me.
They run . . .

Up!

Up.

Up.

and with a push they send me back *up.*

Paper airplane
on a breeze.

Gliding back to Earth.

Gliding across the sandy lot, it stops,

and is noticed by someone.

Someone else . . .

who picks up the airplane.
She brings it to me.
My airplane!

Friends.

"I'm here," says the plane.
"I'm here," says the girl's smile.

Me too. I'm here.

*For the world you may be one person,
but for one person—you may be the world.*

**For Denise and her son, Matthew,
who inspired this story**

This book and the companion film, *I'm here.*, are inspired by the work of the Southwest Autism Research & Resource Center (SAARC), a nonprofit, community-based organization in Phoenix, Arizona, dedicated to providing research, education, and resources for individuals with autism spectrum disorders (ASDs) and their families. Visit autismcenter.org for more information.

For more detailed instructions about how to make a paper airplane, visit the *I'm Here* book page on KIDS.SimonandSchuster.com!

ATHENEUM BOOKS FOR YOUNG READERS
An imprint of Simon & Schuster Children's Publishing Division
1230 Avenue of the Americas, New York, New York 10020

ATHENEUM BOOKS FOR YOUNG READERS is a registered trademark of Simon & Schuster, Inc.
For information about special discounts for bulk purchases, please contact Simon & Schuster Special Sales at 1-866-506-1949 or business@simonandschuster.com.
The Simon & Schuster Speakers Bureau can bring authors to your live event. For more information or to book an event, contact the Simon & Schuster Speakers Bureau at 1-866-248-3049 or visit our website at www.simonspeakers.com.

Book design by Ann Bobco
The text for this book is set in Alghera and Neutraface.
The illustrations for this book are rendered in pen, ink, watercolor, and some digital color.
Manufactured in China
0611 SCP

10 9 8 7 6 5 4 3 2
Library of Congress Cataloging-in-Publication Data
Reynolds, Peter, 1961–
I'm here / Peter H. Reynolds. — 1st ed.
p. cm.
Summary: In a crowded park, a boy makes an airplane out of a piece of paper carried to him by a gentle breeze, sends it on its way, and watches a new friend bring it back to him.
ISBN 978-1-4169-9649-1
[1. Friendship—Fiction. 2. Parks—Fiction. 3. Paper airplanes—Fiction.]
I. Title. II. Title: I am here.
PZ7.R337645Iad 2011
[E]—dc22   2010038962